The diary of
A YOUNG NURSE IN WORLD WAR II

To Mum and Dad, Yvonne and Norma

Editor Louisa Sladen
Editor-in-Chief John C. Miles
Designer Jason Billin/Billin Design Solutions
Art Director Jonathan Hair

First published in 2000
by Franklin Watts
96 Leonard Street
London
EC2A 4XD

Franklin Watts Australia
14 Mars Road
Lane Cove
NSW 2066

ISBN   0 7496 3664 5 (hbk)
0 7496 3945 8 (pbk)

Dewey classification: 941.084

A CIP catalogue record for this book is available
from the British Library.

Printed in Great Britain

The diary of
A YOUNG NURSE IN WORLD WAR II

by Moira Butterfield
Illustrated by Brian Duggan

W
FRANKLIN WATTS
NEW YORK • LONDON • SYDNEY

ALL ABOUT THIS BOOK

This is the fictional diary of Jean Harris, a young trainee nurse in a London hospital during the Second World War (1939-45). During that time London was bombed by the Luftwaffe (the German Air Force), particularly badly between 1940 and 1941 in a period called the Blitz. People living in Britain weren't at the battlefront; instead they were said to be on the "Home Front". This book is about some of the things that happened on the Home Front.

HOW DID THE SECOND WORLD WAR START?

In 1933 Adolf Hitler came to power in Germany, along with his National Socialist Party (they were called Nazis for short). He wanted Germany to conquer many lands and become the most powerful nation in the world. By 1939 he had sent his forces into Austria and Czechoslovakia. Then, on September 1st 1939, his forces invaded Poland. Britain and France felt they could not stand by and let this happen, so, on September 3rd 1939, at 11 am, they declared war on Germany. The countries fighting the Nazis were called the Allies. Germany and the countries that fought alongside her were called the Axis Powers.

How do we know what life was like?

Lots of people who are still alive remember what it was like during the Second World War. Ask your grandparents or any pensioners you know. You'll probably be amazed to hear what they tell you about their past.

Although this diary is made up, much of it is based on real events. Some of these events were described to the author by her own relatives, who were children in wartime London.

For instance, Bobby the dog really did exist. He belonged to the author's great-aunt and made his own way home just as described. A burning plane really did crash just behind the family house, and Canadian soldiers were billeted with the author's grandparents. Those soldiers fought at the battle of Dieppe and sadly only one of them returned alive.

Chapter 1

December 19th 1939
Nurses' Quarters: Hospital in central London

I can't quite believe how much my life has changed in a few short weeks. Just a little while ago I was living at home in West Ealing with Mum and Dad. Now I'm a trainee nurse sharing a room with two other girls I've never met before! My feelings are all mixed up. I'm nervous, excited, worried - I never thought it was possible to feel so many different things at the same time.

I'm going to be pretty busy with work shifts and studying for nursing exams, but when I get the time I'll try to remember to write my diary. I'm determined to do my bit to help make sure Hitler doesn't win this awful war, and I can start by making sure I stay cheerful for all the patients. So Happy Christmas, dear diary. You're going to help keep me smiling for Britain.

My room-mates are both probationary nurses like me. They're called Cessie and Marge and I met them on my first day when we stood waiting to meet Sister Ironside, the Matron in charge.

"Are you nervous? I am!" whispered Cessie. "I'm shaking so much I think my hat might fall off!" admitted Marge. I know I'm going to like them both. Matron arrived, grand and large like a ship in full sail. "Well, come along. Don't stand there gawping like fishes. Someone fetch bed linen, someone tidy the bandage store and someone make me a cup of tea. Three sugars."

There's a jolly hospital porter called Bill and as soon as Matron turned her back he gave a Nazi salute and put a finger under his nose to imitate Hitler's moustache. If Matron had looked round she would have seen us all bursting with silent giggles.

DECEMBER 21ST 1939

We've been at war with Germany since September, but in London you wouldn't know it, except that there are sandbags piled up outside the hospital walls and Matron had us sticking tape over all the windows to stop glass showering in if there are bomb blasts. Oh, and we've got blackout curtains up to stop enemy planes spotting our lights at night. There haven't been any Jerry planes yet but we're expecting them any day.

We've got a hospital volunteer called Mary who was a dressmaker before she signed up to help the war effort. She says Germany will be beaten by summer and then she'll use the blackout curtains to make a glamorous dress for me - just like Ginger Rogers would wear dancing with Fred Astaire in a Hollywood musical. I told her how Fred was my favourite star. She's very kind and good at reassuring me.

"Don't you worry, Jeanie. You'll meet your own Fred one of these days, mark my words."

Marge – Glamorous, isn't she!
All the way from Brighton.

Me – Born and bred in good old London town.

Cessie – Big smile!
Comes from Cardiff.

DECEMBER 23RD 1939
NEARLY CHRISTMAS!

Today Matron told Cessie off for having a ladder in her stockings. "We will keep up our standards, war or no war," she thundered.

Our oldest patient Mr Potter woke up from a doze and said, "Is that Hitler shoutin'?" "No dear, it's Matron," I whispered. "Can't tell the difference," he muttered and went back to sleep.

DECEMBER 25TH 1939
OUR FIRST WARTIME CHRISTMAS

There was a celebration on the wards today. Mr McBride, one of our surgeons, came down from the operating theatre to share some Christmas cake with the nurses. He asked me which movie stars I liked and when I said Fred Astaire he did a dance down between the beds.

"Really, Mr McBride. Standards, you know. Standards!" gasped Matron.

"Lord help Father Christmas when he comes down your chimney, Matron," he chuckled. He's the only one who can get away with teasing her and apparently he does it whenever he gets the chance.

DECEMBER 29TH 1939

I got a note from Mum to say that my sister Vi is evacuating little Irene and Norm in case bombs drop on London. They're being sent up north somewhere and she saw them off at the station with their nametags tied to their wrists and their gas masks in little boxes. Poor things. First their dad goes off to fight and then they get sent away to a faraway strange place where everything gets done differently. That one train journey will turn their world upside-down. I hope they'll get to stay with some kind people.

Chapter 2

JANUARY 20TH 1940
NURSES' QUARTERS

Imagine a nice squidgy chocolate cake, one with icing that squashes out on to your chin when you bite into it. Dear diary, you can tell I'm hungry! Because of the war food imports are right down and rationing has started, to make sure we don't all starve. Everyone got ration books full of coupons for buying basics such as bacon, ham, sugar and butter, but we nurses had to give our coupon books to the hospital because they feed us. At least that's what they call it!

Cessie says at least rationing is one way to lose weight but if it goes on like this someone might mistake me for a bean pole.

We've all agreed that one day we'll go to Hollywood, order a banquet for breakfast and dance in a fountain running with champagne.

That'll be the day!

I'm looking forward to my next day off because I'm going to go home and see the family, and Mum will feed me up.

MARCH 5TH 1940
A LETTER FROM HOME

Dear Jeanie,

Just a quick note to tell you that Vi has brought the children back. She says there isn't much of a war on in London and she couldn't bear to be apart from them, especially as Sid is away with the army in Africa. The kids were evacuated to a farm with some nice kind people and they learnt to catch rats with a ferret. Now Vi says they're trying to train her terrier Bobby to do the same thing along Ealing High Street! My neighbour's kids weren't so lucky, though. She says they were treated like unpaid slaves where they went. Looking forward to seeing you soon. We'll have a big tea!

Love from Mum

I can remember how jealous I was when my big sister left home, married Sid and had kids. Now she's got all that worry, with Sid fighting and the kids to look after in a war. And me? Work has taken over my life. Gotta go. Time for another shift.

MARCH 8TH 1940

Barrage balloons have gone up all over London to block the path of enemy planes. They look like giant silver whales floating on strings. While they're hovering outside, Matron hovers over us inside, making sure we do everything the "correct way", even down to folding the corners of the bedclothes. "Look after the details, girls. Look after the details."

APRIL 10TH 1940

Sorry, diary! I had to miss you for a while. Being a trainee nurse means work, studying, work and then more work. Change that bandage! Empty that bedpan!

We've got a wireless (radio) in the nurses' home and that's how we heard the Nazis have invaded Denmark and Norway. It seems like they're spreading all over Europe, like some awful disease. Will we catch it next?

JUNE 6TH 1940

The Germans have almost taken France and we nearly lost a whole army. The wireless broadcaster said that they were stranded on the beaches of Dunkirk, on the coast of France, with the sea in front of them and the Germans advancing behind. So boats of all shapes and sizes sailed over the Channel from England and brought back hundreds of thousands of soldiers, just in the nick of time. Compared to that my war seems very quiet...

June 10th 1940

Italy has joined with Germany and declared war on us. Mary thinks that Luigi, one of our hospital cooks, will probably be locked up as an enemy alien just because he's Italian, though I don't think he'd hurt a fly. When Mr Potter heard he said: "Is Mussolini comin' 'ere?" and Porter Bill replied: "If he does we'll feed 'im 'ospital food and finish 'im off quick."

June 17th 1940 Black Monday

The whole of France has finally fallen to the Germans and now there's nothing between us and the enemy but a little strip of sea. The Prime Minister, Mr Churchill, came on the wireless and told us to brace ourselves for a 'Battle of Britain', because Hitler will soon send his troops to invade us.

One of the patients had a leaflet about what to do if an invader comes. It said: "Don't give him anything. Don't tell him anything. Hide all food, maps and bicycles." "Do they think 'e's comin' over for a picnic?" someone asked.

I've got my own secret escape route from all

this worry, my private daydream about dancing with Fred Astaire - him in a bow tie and top hat, me in a shimmering dress covered with sequins. Today I even started to waltz down the corridor without thinking, and one of the patients saw me.

"Aye, aye, nurse has bin daydreamin'," he said, when I got back on the ward. "She's dancin' with that invisible Fred again. 'Ere, nurse. Is it nice, your daydream film?"

"Heavenly," I replied.

"Miss Harris!" Matron was standing right behind me and she made me jump a mile. "Kindly keep your mind on your job! I suggest you check the bedpans."

"Never mind, nurse," one of the patients said after she was gone. "There 'as to be a baddie in every movie. Matron's got the part in yours."

THINGS TO DO

Eat more carrots
(to keep healthy and see
better in the blackout)

Read up textbook
on broken bones

Mend stockings (new ones
are getting hard to find)

Think of ways to make
my clothes look more like
Hollywood creations!

Go home Hitler!

Chapter 3

JULY 10TH 1940
BACK FROM MUM AND DAD'S

I finally got time off to go home and visit my family, and I took Cessie with me on the bus. It took ages, winding west through the streets of London. There were no street signs or bus labels anywhere, so if the Germans arrive they won't know which way to go. Good; they won't find my mum and dad!

The old terraced street looked just the same, except for all the blackout curtains in the windows. Mum cooked a lovely tea and must have used up a lot of her food coupons. Real eggs are rationed but, "There's a lot you can do with powdered egg," she insists, and to prove it she showed us her new government cookbook: *Food for the Kitchen Front*. It is supposed to persuade us that things like cabbage and egg powder are just the thing. To make the job harder tea, marge and cooking fat have been added to the ration list. Does that mean Matron will have to give up her daily morning cuppa?

I wonder when we'll see bananas, oranges and lemons in the shops again. They have to come from abroad, of course, but for some reason onions are in short supply too, so they're very expensive. Dad says you can tell a rich man by the onion smell on his breath.

MUM'S 'BEAT THE NAZIS' SCRAMBLED EGG

Feeds 4

2 lb cooked veg
4oz grated cheese
3oz breadcrumbs
2 level tbsp. dried egg mixed with
4 tbsp. water
Chopped parsley
Salt and pepper

Mix everything together in a bowl. Melt some dripping in a frying pan and when it's hot pour the mixture in. Let it cook for 20 minutes, stirring until brown.

Dad's too old to fight but he's an Air Raid Precautions warden (A.R.P. for short) and goes out on patrol making sure people put their lights out at night. He's even dug up his beloved roses to plant vegetables, and painted *Dig for Victory* on his spade handle. As well as veg. there's now an Anderson shelter in the garden, a sort of metal shed buried in a hole. When we hear the air-raid siren go, we're supposed to hurry into the Anderson and wait inside it until the all-clear signal, but if there isn't time to get to it there's a Morrison shelter in the sitting room. You can sit safely inside this metal cage while the house collapses around you, apparently. I don't fancy trying it.

Everyone is nervous in case the Jerry invaders arrive, and old Mr Green next door takes his bayonet out and checks his Anderson for enemies every morning.

Vi and the kids visited while I was at home. Little Norm spent the whole time doing plane impressions, sticking his arms out and screeching down the hallway.

His sister Irene had her dog Bobby all bandaged up with rags. "He's been in a battle but he's won and beaten all the Jerry dogs," she explained. At the moment they're far away from real battles. I hope it stays that way...

On our way home there were no lightbulbs on inside the bus, and we began to feel scared.

We badly wanted to be back in our own room, made welcoming and cosy with our photos of home and loved ones. Those photos help us to hold on to what we know in the face of uncertainty. But in the bus we seemed cut adrift. There was darkness inside, darkness outside, and, who knows, perhaps an enemy just around the corner in the shadows... I'm usually a tough old stick. Things like injections, blood and operations don't bother me. But fear of the unknown, well, that's another matter.

Anderson shelter

July 12th 1940

We had a talk about spies at the hospital today. We've got to be on the lookout for them and not talk about our work in public, or to strangers. "Careless talk costs lives", as the saying goes.

I remember Vi recently got a letter from Sid in Egypt, but he couldn't say much in case spies read the mail. He did tell her the desert was crawling with rats and he had to fight them off with a stick when he went to the outdoor toilet. What would a spy make of that, I wonder? The Germans could spend days trying to decode it!

Still no bombing, but the fear of bombs is always there. Sometimes I look out of my bedroom window at London, good old London, full of historical buildings on every street, each one with an amazing story to tell. Then I think how it would look from the sky, laid out like an open target for a bomber. All those beautiful old churches where people once worshipped in periwigs and frock coats. Those ancient palaces and halls where Henry the Eighth once danced, the inns where Shakespeare drank. They could easily be spotted from the sky and destroyed in minutes - history obliterated in a bomb crater...

JULY 15TH 1940 HOSPITAL GARDENS

Far above our heads there's an almighty fight going on every day. Our RAF pilots are battling with the Luftwaffe, the German air force. Yet most of the time we don't see or hear anything, although today I glanced up and saw some vapour trails left by planes, like white threads stretched and looped across blue silk, the only clue to some deadly invisible duel going on up there. In some hospitals the nurses are caring for the airmen who have been shot down, some of them badly burnt. We haven't had any war casualties yet, and I keep wondering how I would cope if I had to deal with a really bad one...

An old gentleman, one of the patients taking some air, has just come up to me in the garden, and asked why I looked so glum. I told him I was thinking of airmen with burns, their faces perhaps disfigured forever.

"Ah well, we must hope that time will heal their injuries, my dear," he said kindly, patting my hand. "If they live and grow old, some of the marks might fade to kindly wrinkles, though their memories, well, their memories..." He drifted off then, shuffling away through the sunlight. "I saw you chatting with old Colonel Briggs," said Porter Bill when I went back inside. "Nice old gentleman, 'e is. Fought in the last war, I believe. 'E doesn't talk about it though. I suppose 'e's got lots of memories but they're all locked away. Old soldiers are like that."

August 21st 1940

Our Royal Air Force boys have given the
Luftwaffe a real beating. They've won the Battle
of Britain in the skies and Hitler's going to have
to find some other way to beat us. Yesterday Mr
Churchill made a speech on the wireless about it.
His words were very moving - "Never in the
field of human conflict was so much owed by so
many to so few."

Later I saw old Colonel Briggs in the garden
and he waved to me, smiling in the sunshine.
"Good news, nurse! Good news in wartime.
A precious thing."

Norm as a 'plane

SEPTEMBER 12TH 1940
IN THE STOREROOM

I'm catching a quick break in the storeroom, but it's the only one I'll get for a while. War has arrived on our doorstep at last, and it feels something like being in hell. Hitler has been raining bombs down on London since the seventh of this month. First we hear the high-pitched moan of the air-raid sirens, then the droning of the bombers overhead. Then "rat-a-tat-tat", ack-ack guns open fire from below trying to shoot them down, and we hear explosions in the distance.

Now every evening when the sirens go off we get some of the patients into the hospital shelters but others just have to lie under their beds, poor things. We take it in turns to stay with them, listening to the war outside, trying not to panic or to show that we care; trying to seem businesslike and in control, all the while wondering which part of town is getting a pasting. Hoping it won't be us this time.

Most of our old non-war patients have been moved to places in the country. "Lovely mansions and castles, don'tcha know," says Porter Bill. Old Mr Potter and Colonel Briggs will get four-posters, I dare say. I'm glad for their sake. They're better off away from London and the Luftwaffe bombers. Now our wards are filled with blitz casualties, ordinary people whose lives are suddenly turned upside-down by a bomb blast.

⚫━━▭▭▭━◯◯━▭▭▭━━⚫

SEPTEMBER 14TH 1940

Today I treated a woman who had been trapped under the rubble of her home for hours before being dug out. I had to dress her cuts and bruises, but she was frantic to leave. "I need to find my kids," she kept crying. "I don't know where they are. Help me find my kids!" The more she panicked, the more I felt fear overwhelm me and tears welled up in my eyes. What about Norm and Irene? What about Vi and Mum and Dad? Where were they? Dust coated the woman's clothes and was smeared round her eyes and mouth and she screamed and cried until we sedated her. As she lay there sleeping, I tried to calm myself down, fighting the wave of fear racing through my body. Later on, a rescue worker came in with news of her kids, who were safe in someone else's shelter, thank goodness.

⚫━━▭▭▭━◯◯━▭▭▭━━⚫

I waited until I was treating someone for a minor wound, a man with a cut on his head. Then I blurted out the question that was on my mind: "What was it like after the bomb went off?" I wanted to know what people might be going through, but I felt almost too scared to find out.

"Well, we was lucky in our 'ouse because we didn't get a direct 'it, only a bit of damage. We went out into the street and stood around, a bit stunned, like. I remember there was glass all over the floor, like frost crunching under my boots," he replied. "After a while we 'eard trapped people crying out." He seemed matter-of-fact about it all, not cheerful exactly, but in control. "There's no other way, love. I'm still alive, aren't I? So 'carry on', eh? I've gotta get 'ome and 'elp the missus clear up."

SEPTEMBER 20TH 1940
NURSES' QUARTERS

Mary was on her way to work when a raid started last night, so she had to go down to a public shelter in one of the tube stations. "There were hundreds of people sitting on the platforms down there, with kiddies, little babies, even pets, would you believe," she said. "It was very smelly and hot, with lots of lice, and no toilets." It sounds disgusting. I hope I never have to try it down there.

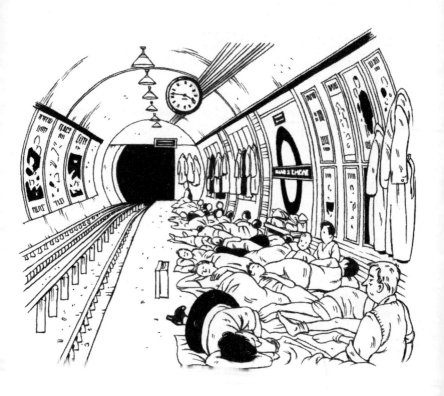

SEPTEMBER 28TH 1940

A mine wiped out a whole street near Mum and Dad's house on the twenty-fifth. The next day the King and Queen visited to see the damage, picking their way over the rubble and trying to find some comforting words for the survivors. I'm so worried the Germans will target the gasworks behind Mum and Dad's house. Porter Bill saw me looking glum. "Come on, Jeanie, don't look on the dark side. Never give up, girl."

He's right. I'm still alive, so "carry on", eh?

OCTOBER 5TH 1940
EVENING ON THE WARD, SITTING WAITING FOR SIRENS

It'll happen again tonight, sure as "eggs is eggs", as Dad would say. Night after night the Nazi bombers pay us a visit as regularly as clockwork.

Some of the bomb victims we're getting in are kids from the East End. They look shocking: so thin and unwashed. Some of them have even got rickets, their legs are all thin and bowed because they've never had enough to eat, not even before the war. I had no idea there were such poor people living right here in my home town. Some of the kids can't read so we teach them the words on the hospital posters - *Walls have Ears* and *Look out in the Blackout.*

NOVEMBER 15TH 1940
HOSPITAL GARDENS

The bombing has stopped in London, though the Germans are bombing other British cities. Poor them. The lull meant that Dad was able to come over to see if I was all right. At home he's been firewatching on the rooftops at night, spotting incendiary bombs. He puts them out with buckets of sand before they smoulder and cause fires.

He brought lots of love from Mum and

cheered me up with his funny stories.
Apparently one of his old neighbours, Mrs Slater, came round the other day. "Buy up knicker elastic," she said. "That's what went short in the last war."

So Dad says: "You've hit on something there, Mrs Slater. Hitler's next secret weapon will be baggy knickers!"

Chapter 4

NOVEMBER 17TH 1940
NURSES' QUARTERS

I don't know what we'd do without the wireless.
We get the news of course, but there are some
funny programmes on and lovely music too.
One of the patients told me he was a good
dancer and would teach me to tap-dance like
Fred Astaire and Eleanor Powell in *Broadway
Melody*. Only this bloke's name is Harold, not
Fred, and he's got his leg in a cast. When I

pointed this out he said,
"All right then. You do
the dance moves and
I'll sit 'ere and tap
my cast on the floor.
That way you'll
sound just like the
real thing."

survive anything you can do."

There's been a little miracle at home too. Bobby, Irene and Norm's dog, has turned up! Someone found him sitting on the bombsite that was his old home. He'd walked miles from Mum's, all on his own, back to the place he knew - where Vi's house had been. A neighbour in the old street has agreed to look after him. The kids were upset at first that he wasn't coming back to live with them at Mum and Dad's. But they felt better when Dad said that Bobby was a real war hero, showing us all how to be brave and overcome hardship. Irene says she is going to write to Mr Churchill about him. Good for her!

I haven't seen the real thing in ages because at the moment we don't get time off. I hardly get time to sleep or eat, let alone get dressed up and go to the cinema.

"Don't forget we're going to Hollywood when the war's over," Marge reminded me. "We'll wear our best clothes - hats, gloves, everything! We'll go dancing and we'll take Bing Crosby for Cessie, Frank Sinatra for me and Fred Astaire for you, Jean."

"I'll come, too," said Porter Bill. "And make sure you fix me up with Ginger Rogers, or I'll 'ave to bring Matron along. She could get a part in a movie ... as the bride of Frankenstein! She'd rise up from her coffin, all red-eyed and staring, shouting: 'Clean this up at once, nurse!'

DECEMBER 14TH 1940
LETTER FROM MUM

Dear Jean,

I'm sorry to tell you that Vi's house was hit. Vi and the kids were in the shelter with the dog so they're safe, thank goodness, but there's nothing left of the house. They've come to stay with me and Dad, but little Norm and Irene are desperate because their dog Bobby disappeared from here yesterday. He got out of our garden and hasn't been seen since. I'm sorry you're too busy to come home for Christmas. Good luck with your nursing exams.

We'll be thinking of you.

Love from Mum

Now I feel utterly desperate myself. I'm working night shifts all over Christmas, with no time off, so there will be no chance of seeing Vi and the kids. If they hadn't been in the shelter when the bomb dropped... I'd better stop writing before that wave of fear crashes over me again.

DECEMBER 25TH 1940
WARTIME CHRISTMAS NO. 2

Christmas should be cheerful, despite everything, so Cessie, Marge and me decided to do a little song for the patients. We practised singing:

"HEY! LITTLE HEN! WHEN, WHEN, WHEN
WILL YOU LAY A LITTLE EGG FOR ME?
HEY! LITTLE HEN! WHEN, WHEN, WHEN,
WILL YOU TRY TO SUPPLY ONE FOR ME?"

Then we did it for the whole ward, only we didn't realise that Matron had come in and wa standing behind us. She didn't say anything a all; just raised an eyebrow.

"Come on, Sister, your turn," shouted one the cheekier patients. "How about the dance the seven veils? All sexy, like."

"Time for your bedbath, Mr Smith," Mat replied in her most threatening voice.

DECEMBER 31ST 1940

On the 29th there was the worst bombing yet. The City of London, one of London's areas, burned to the ground, all except S Paul's Cathedral. It stood firm as flames around it, defiant, as if the spirits of the were sending a message to Hitler: "We

Chapter 5

JANUARY 4TH 1941 NURSES' QUARTERS

I am aching with tiredness. The bombing goes on night after night, and the war news isn't good, either. Lectures and exams have been delayed. "You will have to learn as you work, girls," Matron says.

Needed: An excuse for a bit of fun!

Coming up soon: Marge's birthday.
Remember and plan: – Cake?
Present? Somehow!

JANUARY 10TH 1941
MARGE'S BIRTHDAY!

How old is Marge? She won't say! My guess is she's twenty. We couldn't manage a real birthday cake but Mary brought in a dummy version made out of a hat box, with real candles on the top for Marge to blow out. I gave her a tin of peaches as a present because they're such a luxury.

Must go. Marge is opening her can and has promised to give me a peach slice!

JANUARY 30TH 1941

Fred Astaire has got a new film out, but I don't know when I'll manage to see it.

"Tell you what, Jeanie. We'll find you a Fred of your own,"said Porter Bill, and he asked the patients if they knew anybody of that name. "I know a bloke with a dog called Fred," one of them replied. "Can he dance?" Bill asked. "The bloke can't, but the dog does a lovely two-step," came the reply. My life is work, work, work, so if Fred Astaire himself walked in and asked me on a date I wouldn't have time to go!

Sugar is in very short supply so we had to use treacle in Matron's tea today. Tea leaves are short, too, but Matron seems to have a secret supply of tea leaves, more than her ration,

I would say. It's a mystery where she gets them from, but at least we could give Fred Astaire a cuppa if he dropped by, even if we're too busy to go dancing with him.

FEBRUARY 5TH 1941

Jerry's dropping something new on us - exploding incendiaries. Ordinary ones can be smothered in sand or picked up with heavy gloves and carried away, but the new booby-trapped versions explode when they're touched. The trouble is, you can't tell just by looking whether a bomb is booby-trapped or not.

Still, as Dad says, when your number's up, it's up. You can't go round worrying about it. If you see an incendiary you've got to take your chance and try to put it out. If it's booby-trapped, well, you'll have died doing something brave.

I've just reread what I've written and it all sounds very calm. It's that "keep a brave face on it" war talk we all use to keep us going. I don't know how I'd really feel face to face with a bomb.

I've got some letters and drawings from home which will go in my precious diary. That way I'll never lose them, and I'll be able to reread them when I'm an old lady – if Hitler lets me get that far!

Dear Auntie Jean,

I hope you are well. Grandma says you are working very hard and you are very brave. Our school days are often stopped by air-raid sirens. We have to collect our books and go into the school shelter. I don't like it because it smells. We have got a Belgian refugee boy in our class. His family were driven out by the Nazis and they all crossed the sea in a really small boat.

All the children in our class like to collect shrapnel from the ground after an air raid. As soon as the all clear goes we go out to get it. Norm has an empty brass shell case which is the best find so far. We have to keep a spoon at school to get our cod liver oil dose from the government. We also have a rug each because it gets cold. My friend Ann had a jar of chocolate powder from America. We dipped our fingers in it and licked them. There are not many books at school so I have read the same ones over and over.

Much love from Irene

Chapter 6

MAY 11TH 1941

In bed. Can't sleep! I'll never forget last night as long as I live. In the evening, wave after wave of bombers kept coming over, more than I've ever heard before. The lights went out in the operating theatre and Mr McBride had to finish his operation by candlelight. That wasn't the worst of it, though. About two o'clock in the morning, only Matron and I were left on the ward, seeing to the patients we couldn't move to the shelter. As I held a patient's hand I heard a tell-tale "plop" noise on the roof above my head, then silence. I knew there and then it was an incendiary bomb.

Matron had heard it too. She spoke to me quietly : "Please come with me, Miss Harris." We walked along the ward to the storeroom where we could talk privately.

Chapter 7

MAY 13TH 1941 NURSES' QUARTERS

Peaceful! The bombing has stopped, thank
goodness. Now I can catch up on my diary. I
don't know why Hitler has called off his planes.
I suppose he's got some other evil plan up his
sleeve and we'll find out what it is all too soon.

MAY 26TH 1941

Terrible news. HMS *Hood*, our biggest
battleship, has been sunk. The German *Bismarck*
intercepted her and scored a hit on the ship's
magazine, where they kept all the torpedoes.
The *Hood* blew up and sank in just a few
minutes. Apparently there were over a
thousand men on board. It's an awful setback.
Churchill has ordered our naval forces to

hunt down the *Bismarck* and destroy her, come what may.

MAY 28TH 1941

The Royal Navy has sunk the *Bismarck*. Our ships chased her and caught her on the way to France. A cheer went up when it was announced on the ward, though they say two thousand German sailors were killed. It's us or them, I suppose. How strange life is in wartime. In the hospital we work hard to save lives, yet people cheer when enemy lives are lost. How would I feel nursing an enemy soldier? Matron says nurses must treat all humans, whatever their beliefs. "We must do what we can for anyone who walks through the doors of this hospital." She's a funny old stick - a mixture of "hard-as-nails" and "help the human race". Is that the ideal nurse?

Cessie, Marge and I have been talking about it and though we can't decide what makes the perfect nurse, there's one thing we all agree on. Because of the war a lot more women are working than ever before, earning their own money and doing important jobs. If we win the war we want things to stay that way.

"Blimey. Women are plottin' to take over!" Porter Bill says. "Come to think of it, that might not be so bad!"

JUNE 24TH 1941

Hitler has attacked Russia and that's why London's been left alone - all his bomber planes are busy over there. I hope this time the Nazis have bitten off more than they can chew, and the Russians defeat them.

Meanwhile, back on the Home Front clothes rationing has started. We've all got ration books with coupons inside for buying clothes, and we've got to "make do and mend" so the things we've got last as long as possible. Mrs Slater was right about the knicker elastic. Porter Bill says he'll make his old socks last a bit longer and then he'll get them dropped on Hitler as a secret weapon!

JULY 5TH 1941

Mum and Dad have got three Canadian soldiers billeted with them! They're doing a three-week signals course at the local college before they go off to their army bases. I got home as soon as I could to meet the new arrivals. They're all over six feet tall and very gentlemanly! One of them has made a couple of toy ships for Norm out of scrap wood, and now Norm can have naval battles on the sitting room carpet and sink the *Bismarck* every night.

One of the Canadians asked me if I'd like to go to a dance with him. A dance! I can hardly remember how. I promised to ask Cessie and Marge as partners for his friends.

"Oi, Jean. Is this Canadian of yours called Fred by any chance?" asked Porter Bill, when I got back to work. I wouldn't tell him (though between you and me, his name's Rick).

"That's for me to know and you to find out," I said. "You can call him Mr X."

"Blimey, you'd think I was a spy!" Bill laughed. "Do you think I might report back to 'itler on your love life?"

JULY 8TH 1941 NURSES' QUARTERS

I've never seen Marge and Cessie so excited! We've spent ages getting our clothes right for the dance. Marge has run out of belts and there aren't any on sale, so she's made one out of paper for her dress. We've been using a couple of ideas from Marge's magazine, which is full of tips on how to cheat the shortages. I must write some of them down in case I need them.

Paint legs to look as if you're wearing stockings.

Use bicarbonate of soda under the armpits as an anti-perspirant.

Use burnt cork as eyelash mascara.

Use beetroot juice and water as fake lipstick, with vaseline on top.

To be honest, I don't think I'll be painting my lips with beetroot juice!

JULY 9TH 1941

The dance was a great success. Rick was a good dancer and the time seemed to fly by in a blur of music. He told me about his home, where the snow can fall six feet deep sometimes. He's even trapped bears! "We don't get those much in London," I said. "Don't be so sure. I've heard a bear once left pawprints in Piccadilly," he joked. "Next time it snows, we'll go there together and hunt for one."

We were having such a lovely evening we forgot the time. So after our goodbyes, Marge, Cessie and I raced back to the nurses' home, only to find that the gates were locked for the night. "Come on, we'll climb over them," whispered Marge, so we hitched up our dresses, tucked them up around our waists and climbed over the fence, trying not to giggle. We had a scare when a man walked past but he kept his hat pulled down over his eyes and pretended not to see us. It was quite easy getting over the gates really. Just as well we weren't enemy invaders! I wonder what that man was doing out so late. Come to think of it, he could have been spying!

I'm feeling cheerful. Dancing does you good! More nursing exams soon, though...

⊶⫘▯▯▭◯◯▭▯▯⫘⊷

JULY 14TH 1941

I keep thinking about dancing with Rick, and how handsome he was. What colour were his eyes exactly? Did he like me? Did I step on his toes too many times? Can you fall in love at first sight? I hope I know more answers than this when it comes to my exam questions tomorrow!

July 14th 1941

Exam — 2pm, main hall

Concentrate!

August 1st 1941

Dear Jeanie,

We've been sent off to our British bases — top secret destinations I'm afraid. I'm sorry I couldn't get to see you again but I'm going to write whenever I can.

Think of me next time it snows, and look out for bears.

With fond goodbyes

Rick

Chapter 8

DECEMBER 8TH 1941
CHRISTMAS IS COMING!

Oops! I've been so busy I forgot to write! Well, all right, the truth is that in between working I've been writing to Rick, and though I don't know where he's stationed I'm hoping my letters will reach him through the war office. But now I have big news so I must keep a record of it. With no warning, Japan, an ally of Germany, attacked the American navy at Pearl Harbor in the Pacific, and that was enough for America to join the war on our side.

"Get ready girls, the Yanks are coming!" said Porter Bill. "They'll be wanting some dance partners, that's for sure!"

I wonder what they'll think when they see the state we're in. The queues for food and clothing get longer and longer, though that's good news for black marketeers, who secretly sell off stolen supplies of things like petrol. I hadn't come across it until yesterday, when a man tapped me on the shoulder in the ward. He was in to visit his dad. "Psst, nurse," he whispered. "Have these, love." He handed me a small package with a lipstick and a pair of silk stockings inside. "Early Christmas present. A thank-you for looking after Dad. No questions asked, all right?" he said, and hurried off, pulling his hat down over his eyes.

It was obvious they were black market – stolen goods. Mary said that everyone gets things on the black market if they can, so I should keep them and say nothing. "Where do you think Matron gets her extra tea leaves?" she said. Of course! The man in the hat outside the hospital that night after the dance... He was Matron's secret black market tea leaf supplier. Or am I confusing life with the movies? As usual!

DECEMBER 25TH 1941
WARTIME CHRISTMAS NO. 3

How long will the war go on?

Mr McBride brought his usual Christmas cake down for the nurses but, because of rationing, it was a strange mixture made from soaked prunes and condensed milk. As usual, he teased Matron.

"Tell me, how do you stay so well fed?" he asked. "Have you got a boyfriend who's in the black market?" "Mr McBride!" she cried, as usual. I love Christmas!

December 26th 1941

Yesterday, on Christmas Day of all days, our colony in Hong Kong surrendered to the enemy Japanese. A lot of nurses were out there, and they'll probably go to prisoner-of-war camps. I felt so cheerful yesterday, partly because I somehow thought I might get some message from Rick. But I didn't. Life isn't a movie after all. This war is like being on a roller-coaster at the fair. First you're up, then, in the blink of an eye, you plunge down. Did Rick get any of my letters? Has he forgotten me already?

January 7th 1942

I got a note from Rick!

Dear Jean,

Hi! I can't say where I am or what I'm doing! Good letter, eh? One thing I am allowed to say – I can't stop thinking about you! I hope you're ok. How's the training going? I got your letters and I can't tell you how much they mean to me. Matron sounds as fierce as a sergeant–major!
Keep writing.

Love,

Rick

March 5th 1942

The Americans have arrived. I saw some of them strolling along the street, tall and smiling and flirting. "Hey babe, you look cute." "Honey, give me a smile."

One of them gave me some chewing gum. I've never even seen such a thing before! It was like someone handing me a rare jewel.

A couple of days later we went to an American GI dance and we came home with our handbags full of chewing gum. This morning the ward echoed to the thunderous tones of Matron: "You will NOT chew gum in this hospital!"

One of the soldiers had a leaflet that he let me keep. I've written out some of it here.

IMPORTANT DO'S AND DON'TS FOR AMERICAN SOLDIERS IN BRITAIN

Be friendly but don't intrude anywhere it seems you are not wanted.

If you are invited to eat with a family don't eat too much. Otherwise you might eat up their weekly rations...

Don't make wisecracks about British defeats.

Never criticise the King or Queen.

Never say "I look like a bum."

Marge says they should add a line - "Never upset Matron."

MAY 8TH 1942
A LETTER FROM IRENE

Dear Auntie Jean,

I hope you are well. You haven't visited for ages. Grandma says you've been busy with work. Come soon. Now there are no more bombs Mum lets us out to play outside a bit more in the evenings. Norm is in the Cubs and he is collecting waste paper to get a badge. I hope to get a badge by collecting old books. Mrs Slater's daughter is going out with an American soldier called Hank. He is very nice and gives us cigarette cards because we are collecting them. He gives us sweets and chewing gum, too.

Mum says Dad has been winning the war in Africa. His bit of the army is called the Desert Rats. My Dad is one of the rats!

Lots of love, Irene

SEPTEMBER 16TH 1942

I've been neglecting my diary. I've been trying to avoid putting my fears down in black and white, but I think now that I should try to face them. I'm desperately worried about Rick. Canadian troops left Britain to fight at Dieppe in August. They took an awful beating and a lot of them were killed or taken prisoner.

Marge says he's sure to find a way to let me know he's all right. But what if he doesn't? What if I don't hear anything from him at all?

OCTOBER 8TH 1942

In an ordinary world we'd be qualifying as nurses now. But it's not an ordinary world and our training's been delayed by all the bombing. It feels like my whole life has been delayed, freeze-framed on the screen. The picture's stopped and won't move again until I hear from Rick.

DECEMBER 1ST 1942

I went home to Mum and Dad's, hoping to hear news of Rick, but there wasn't any.

While I was waiting for the bus back to hospital I've been counting all the government posters on the street corners, telling us what we

should and shouldn't do... Don't waste food,
behave properly in the shelters, look out in the
blackout, carry your gas mask, join up for this
and that, dig for victory, knit for the troops,

careless talk costs lives, is your journey really necessary? Coughs and sneezes spread diseases... They should print one that says: *Don't Fall in Love with Soldiers*.

I'm tired of the blackout, tired of being hungry, tired of the air-raid sirens and the bombs that still fall once in a while, tired of the constant fear that's come back to hide in the back of my brain, waiting to jump out and catch me unawares. Even my Hollywood dream is wearing threadbare, and I can't find a new one.

DECEMBER 25TH 1942
WARTIME CHRISTMAS NO. 4

I thought to myself that a dusting of snow might be nice this year, just a thin white blanket thrown over our lovely damaged old town one night to make it seem new and sparkling for a few hours, before the snowflakes turn to slush and splash my shoes.

But there's no snow, and there'll be no bear-hunting in Piccadilly.

Ever.

Chapter 9

MAY 8TH 1943 HOSPITAL GARDENS

I'm sitting on a bench out in the gardens, and everything is beginning to flower again, so it seems a good time to bring my diary out again. I put it away for a while, along with all my hopes.

So life goes on, but there are so many shortages now it's getting quite comical. We've hardly any crockery left on the wards and Matron has to drink her tea from a shaving mug.

Porter Bill went to a newsagents the other day and the girl behind the counter had a cardboard sign round her neck saying "No Cigarettes", because she was so fed up with people asking for them. Everyone has useful suggestions for "making do" - flour sacks for curtains, coffee made out of dandelion roots ...sounds disgusting. There are some things you just can't fake, though. Today a patient asked me to pull the curtains round his bed and then whispered, very secretively, in my ear.

"Nurse, have you got any whisky? For medicinal purposes, like. Only I haven't had a drop in months. I reckon someone's bin hoardin' the nation's supply."

"Who would hoard all the whisky?" I asked.

"I dunno who it is, but I wish 'e lived near me," sighed the poor man and slumped back on his pillow, resigned to Bovril in a cup with its handle missing.

Cessie and Marge are asking if they can write in my diary.

Roses are red
violets are blue
Marge is the tops
and Jean is too!

Hollywood
here we come!

Love Cessie XX

wot no beer?

JULY 15TH 1943

We've qualified. At last. What will happen next? Will Cessie go back to Wales, and Marge to Brighton? I'll miss them dreadfully if they do. In the meantime we're going to toast ourselves tonight with "hospital champagne" (that's Bovril to you and me).

JULY 17TH 1943

Cessie, Marge and me have decided to stay together if we can and see this war through in London. There are more and more wounded soldiers being sent to the hospital, so there's lots to do. We hear about the war from them, snippets of stories that make faraway place names and battles suddenly seem up-close. In the back of my mind I have a tiny spark of hope that news of Rick will arrive. It's only tiny, and it's getting fainter all the time.

SEPTEMBER 15TH 1943

Yesterday I went home and stepped straight into some high excitement. Mum, Vi and me were standing at the back door, and the kids were playing in the back garden, when suddenly our heads jerked up. We stood in frozen horror as something shot over the roof, shooting out flames and missing the chimney by inches.

We didn't realise it was a plane at first and it crossed my mind that it was a new weapon. It crashed with an almighty crunch into the coke heaps beyond the gasworks at the back of the house. If it had hit the works we'd all have died there and then.

"Blimey!" cried Dad, running out of his shed to see what the noise was. "Wow!' cried the kids, as the wreckage went up in a ball of flame. Next, the whole neighbourhood was out in the street, chattering excitedly.

"Was it one of ours?"

"I didn't see."

"Did the crew bail out?"

"They might be Luftwaffe!"

"Let's look for 'em!"

"Watch it! They could be armed!"

Well, in the end we found out it was one of ours, and the crew had bailed out safely. There were no Huns hiding in the potting sheds, but it was the closest Mum and Dad's house has come to being destroyed.

Here's hoping their luck holds out.

SEPTEMBER 20TH 1943

I've just found out that Irene and Norm got over the wall into the gasworks as soon as they could after the aeroplane crash near home. Norm picked up a belt of unused ammunition and would have brought it home for his little shrapnel collection if Dad hadn't realised where the kids had gone. He rushed over to get them and took the live bullets away to hand in to the Home Guard.

Norm is very grumpy and thinks he should have been allowed to keep the bullets. He says he knew a boy who took a whole bomb into school on the back of his bike. When the teacher saw it they all had to go outside until someone came to defuse it. What a hair-raising story!

Must go. Busier than ever.

December 25th 1943
Wartime Christmas No. 5

This year Mr McBride brought us a cake made from carrots. We had a good sing-song and lots of silly jokes, but no presents for each other. Marge gave me an IOU instead.

> *Christmas 1943*
>
> *To Jean Harris,*
>
> *I OU one Christmas present.*
> *To be collected after the war.*
> *Won't it be a surprise!*
>
> *Marge Philips*

Dear Auntie Jean,

Thank you for the present. I was sorry you could not get time off to come home for Christmas. I got a painting book, a game of cards and the handkerchief you sent. Norm got a set of jacks, the scarf you sent and a train made from empty tins. We were very lucky because we had an orange to share! I saved my pieces all day. Now they're gone but I've put the nice-smelling peel under my pillow. For lunch we had corned beef hash and wartime Christmas pudding that Gran says she made from carrots. It was all right, though. We listened to the radio and played games.

Mum says that now Dad has helped to beat the Germans in Africa he might be able to come home next Christmas. Last time I saw him he had white knees but Mum says they will be brown now. I can't wait to see.

Lots of love,

Irene

Dear Auntie Jean,

Thank you for my scarf. I helped Grandad paint fir cones to decorate our house for Christmas. I would have liked some chocolate but the sweet shop had no supplies, only a pretend bar in the window and it was made of wood. I was worried Father Christmas would not find his way here in the blackout but he did. I got a train that Grandad made from tins. It looks very good.

Love from Norm.

PS: Happy New Year, Jeanie! Love from Mum, Dad and Vi.

Those kids have been separated from their dad for ages. I wonder if Norm even remembers a Christmas with Sid. He was only a toddler when his dad signed up and marched off to fight. He probably remembers the little things, like his dad's bristly chin and his chuckling laugh. Funny how you remember little things... like dance music, funny jokes, holding hands...

Chapter 10

FEBRUARY 20TH 1944
HOSPITAL CANTEEN

Here's a typical snippet of the talk to be heard in the hospital canteen at the moment:

"The Nazis have had it."

"Don't you believe it. The closer we get to victory, the harder Jerry will fight."

"Have you heard about this new wonder drug called penicillin? They're using it on the troops in Europe."

"They need all the help they can get."

"I wonder what it must be like living in Germany. Wretched, I shouldn't wonder."

It seems the war is going our way at last, but nobody is quite sure when it will end.

I long for it to finish.

April 20th 1944

Mr McBride has had a wonderful idea. He realised that everyone was feeling a bit war-weary and we needed something to keep us going, so he's suggested that the hospital staff start to plan a bit of a show. "Nothing too grand; just an entertainment that we can put on for the staff and patients when the time is right."

We all thought it was a fantastic idea and brightened up straight away. Even Matron was heard to say she likes a show - "In the correct place and at the correct time."

May 20th 1944

Plans for the show are going slowly but surely. Those of us who want to take part are keeping quiet about it until we feel a bit more confident. Porter Bill says he's going to practise a comic routine. I've decided I am going to work on a dance routine, as if I were Fred Astaire's latest screen partner, Rita Hayworth. Can I persuade Marge and Cessie to be my backing singers? And what about a costume?

I need a plan!

How can I make my shoes sound like tap shoes? Glue on washers? I'd better experiment.

JUNE 6TH 1944 NURSES' QUARTERS

This morning Marge eagerly called me outside to look at the sky. "Look, Jean! Planes! As far as the eye can see!"

The sky was filled with our aircraft towing gliders (the gliders were filled with our troops, we guessed). Plane after plane went by, glinting like silver dragonflies in the sun as they headed for Europe. Look out, Hitler, here we come!

June 8th 1944

All the American GIs have gone with the invasion force and there are no more dance partners or chewing gum. But we don't miss the dances too much. As long as everything stays quiet over here, we should be able to put the show on in a couple of months! Bill said I should have a Fred Astaire look-alike dancing with me on stage, but I'm not going to. There's no one at the hospital young enough or handsome enough. Besides, no one can dance as well as Rick could. I'd rather dance on my own.

June 20th 1944
In the Hospital Shelter

I'm writing this down in the hospital bomb shelter again. We should have known Hitler would have a surprise up his sleeve for us. A horrible nightmare of a surprise. He's started sending over a new weapon, a flying bomb. It's like the Blitz again but without the planes. They're calling the bombs "buzz bombs" or "doodle-bugs". You can hear them coming because their engines make a "phut phut" noise. Then they go quiet and you know they're going to fall. We're rushed off our feet with casualties. It's awful. We can forget putting on the show for a while.

July 5th 1944

I've been told to rest. I'm not allowed to work today. I thought I'd been through it all, until this morning when I had an hour's break and went out to get some fresh air. I heard it before I saw it...the "cough-cough" sound of a small engine in the sky. Above me flew a sinister long shape with fins, like some strange underwater creature that had lost its way. Then it went silent, and the silence was truly terrifying. It meant that the flying bomb was about to fall, perhaps on me.

I was paralysed, listening for a sound, any sound. "Keep flying, keep flying," I muttered. Then, "Quick, duck!" I heard someone cry and an arm pulled me down. The ground shook with a huge explosion and I felt my hair being blown about in a rush of wind. My eyes were shut tightly, but I heard a hollow whistle above my head. As it faded away I opened my eyes and looked around to find that the bomb had completely destroyed a savings bank much further along the road, leaving a space in the street like a tooth missing from an open mouth. Dust floated down on the street around me, carpeting everything. "It looks like snow in summer," I thought to myself. "War snow." Rick flashed into my mind. Then I noticed there were no leaves left on the trees. I fainted.

July 8th 1944

I am feeling much better. The ringing in my ears has nearly stopped. I'm still shaken but my little brush with a bomb is nothing compared to what the troops are going through in Europe and the Far East, where the fighting is very fierce. Sid is in the thick of it somewhere in Italy, apparently.

The patients have all been very kind to me on my return to the ward. "Good to see you back, love. I missed those Hollywood tunes you're always humming."

November 12th 1944

There's another kind of bomb coming over London, one with no warning noise. The first you know about it is a big flash in the sky. Then there's an enormous explosion straight afterwards. It's a terrible new kind of weapon called a V2.

It seems as if the war might be over soon, yet these V2s are still coming over and people are still dying in the streets. How awful it would be to lose someone you love with the end of the fighting just around the corner.

V1 " Doodlebug "

V2
rocket

Chapter 11

DECEMBER 23RD 1944

Rehearsal time today. We've had freezing fog outside and dried egg omelettes for lunch, but we don't care because it's almost time for our show. We're doing it in the canteen on the twenty-seventh. Our costumes are ready, our lines are learnt and my dance steps are just about perfect. Move over, Rita Hayworth!

DECEMBER 28TH 1944

What a night I've just had. It was made even more exciting and breathtaking by the years of dreary war I've been through. I feel as if I've woken up from a half-sleep and everything has come to life in glorious technicolour. I love Christmas!

I must write down what I remember, while

it's fresh in my mind. Our audience for the show were patients and staff. They cheered and clapped as we stood in the corridor outside, waiting for the performance to begin in the canteen. I should have realised something was up when I saw Dad arrive and go over to talk to Porter Bill. I was surprised to see him but I was glad he'd made the effort to come. I didn't think about it again because I was busy being nervous, going over my act in my head.

First on stage was Mr McBride, very smart in a bow tie and tails. He was very funny, introducing each act and saying lots of cheeky things about Matron, as usual.

"Matron, can you go and finish Hitler off? Walk up behind him and shout 'Bedbath'!"

"Mr McBride!" boomed a familiar voice from the audience, but it sounded friendly.

Then Porter Bill and Mary came on and did a comedy routine.

"I say, I say. I went to the museum today."

"To see an ancient relic?"

"No, my mother-in-law stayed at home!"

After that one of the cooks did some magic tricks. He had a black hat made out of cardboard boxes and a string of flags made from bandages. Then he pretended to saw a theatre nurse in half.

At last it was our turn.

"And now, three lovely ladies who came to train way back in 1939, and have since turned into three fine nurses, a credit to this hospital. Announcing... Matron's treasures, Marge, Cessie and Jean, as Rita Hayworth and her Hawaiian babes!"

My stomach did a double somersault as we walked on stage. Mr McBride put the record on and we began to sing and dance along to it. The music carried me along and I began to really enjoy myself! I didn't look at the audience but they must have enjoyed it because they whooped and hollered for more at the end.

We were about to go off stage when Mr McBride grabbed me.

"Jean, or should I say Rita," he said. "It seems a shame that you have to dance on your own without Fred Astaire. But there's someone here tonight who wants to help out. It's someone you haven't seen in a while. He was badly wounded in battle and couldn't contact you; but he's recovered and returned to your parents' home this week to find you. Your dad has brought him tonight, and I believe his name is Mr X, otherwise known as Rick, which he tells me is short for Frederick!"

At that Rick walked on, to deafening cheers. Someone put another record on and we danced together there and then. Other people joined us and danced, too. It was like a dream, as if I'd finally stepped into my own personal Hollywood movie, entitled: *The Best Moment of My Life*.

September 15th 1945
Hospital Gardens

I realise I've forgotten to write my diary at all for a while. So much has happened: you could say I've been swept off my feet. Well, there's a little bit of space at the back of this notebook and I ought to finish the story, so I'll have something to remember: the good times as well as the bad.

After Christmas 1944 the war dragged on for a while, with Germany and Japan still fighting in Europe and the Far East, though we were pretty certain we'd won. We could put the lights on again and tear down the blackout material (which, to Matron's horror, came off in a shower of dust and dead insects).

The bombing has stopped for good, but London looks an awful dirty mess. It will take a long time to fill up those gaping holes and rubble-strewn wastelands where buildings once stood. Bananas and oranges haven't magically appeared in piles along with truckloads of chocolate, new clothes and real eggs... I guess all those things will take a long, long time. But I think it's magical that London is still standing.

"Staggering a bit, but still standing," Porter Bill says.

On May 1st we heard the news that Hitler had killed himself.

"Good riddance," people muttered as it came

over the wireless; then they went quiet, taking it in I suppose. The enemy really was beaten.

Then there was one of those amazing days that will stay in people's memories forever. We'd been waiting and waiting for news of the final surrender, every day thinking it might come. Then, on the afternoon of May 8th, we were busy on the ward when Matron rushed in, clapping her hands excitedly like a little girl.

"My dears! The war is over. Mr Churchill has just announced it. It's VE Day! Victory in Europe!" Cheers went up from the patients and people hugged and shook hands. Later on, we were able to go outside where the streets were thronging with people singing, cheering, climbing up lamp-posts, kissing strangers, dancing jigs and crying out...

"We beat 'em!"

"I can hardly believe it's over."

"Things will never be the same, that's for sure. We'll get bananas now!"

Before we knew it Cessie, Marge and I found ourselves picked up and whirled around by soldiers, and we jumped up and down, whooping like kids when someone tied a Union Jack to a tree.

And do you know what the strangest, most amazing part of that day was? Matron actually hugged me!

SEPTEMBER 20TH 1945

There's more to tell. More partying, but sadly, more deaths and horror. The war wasn't over in the Far East, but we seemed to forget about that in London until we heard the news in August that Japan had surrendered. Actually, what was more of a shock was the news that the Americans used two new weapons called atomic bombs. They dropped them on the Japanese and wiped out two whole cities. I don't know much about how they work, but thank God Hitler didn't ever get hold of them to use on us.

***

We had another party on what people called VJ Day, short for Victory in Japan, and we heard a broadcast from the King, who began by saying: "The war is over."

"Thank gawd," one of the patients said, but it was all quite subdued compared to VE Day. People were horrified that the atomic bomb had been used, and we'd already had our big victory party for the end of the war in Europe. In the end it was a quiet finish to all those years of war. I felt I was one of the lucky ones. I'd survived and ended the war with the person I loved the most.

Chapter 12

MARCH 7TH 1946 ON THE HIGH SEAS!

I'm writing this on board the biggest ship I've ever seen, on my way to Canada with Mum and Dad. Fred has asked me to visit, and I'm going to see if I like it and to find out about nursing over there. I was sad to say goodbye to all my friends at the hospital, though they gave me a really good send-off. I've promised to write lots of letters and Cessie and Marge have promised to come and visit me if I decide to stay in Canada.

The family were there to see us off at the quayside. There was Sid, home from the war and full of stories good and bad about spitting camels and surrendering Germans. When he got home Vi said the kids stared at him for a moment, a deeply suntanned man who didn't look quite like the dad they remembered. Then he chuckled and they knew it was him. Vi said she didn't care what he looked like. She still loved him! They stood on the dockside together, while Norm and Irene jumped up and down, waving madly. Even Bobby the dog was there, barking at the commotion.

Mum and Dad are with me on the boat. Dad said they both needed a break from powdered egg and cardboard chocolate, and they want to see what I might be letting myself in for. I'm longing to see Fred and Canada, though I will miss the kids, Vi and Sid, London, even Matron!

Mum asked me a funny question today as we walked along the deck. "You know what Fred said about Canadian bears. Well, just how big are they?"

"Don't worry, Mum," I replied. "Fred says that if I can handle Matron I can handle a grizzly any day!"

Cessie and Marge say goodbye

Me, Mum and Dad get a banana!

Our Wedding Day – July 27th 1946

Time to get a new diary!

WHAT HAPPENED NEXT

After the war life in Britain was still difficult for a while. There was less meat than ever and bread was in short supply too. Clothes rationing didn't end until 1949; petrol rationing ended in 1950 and food rationing finally ended in 1954. Four million houses, a third of all British homes, had been damaged during the bombings and half a million had been totally destroyed, so there was a lot of rebuilding to do.

Over in America and Canada there had never been rationing, so the shops were well stocked. Jean and her parents, visiting from Europe, would have been amazed to see the stores filled with luxuries.

In defeated Germany life was very difficult, and people had to rebuild their lives slowly. Some Nazi leaders were put on trial for war crimes such as the mass murder of Jewish people.

After the war, part of Germany was occupied by the Allied forces, and part was occupied by Russian troops. Eventually it was split into two countries, Democratic West Germany and Communist East Germany, and it stayed that way until 1990, when the two countries reunited. Now Germany is an ally of Britain and a partner in the European Union.

WORLD WAR TWO -
SOME IMPORTANT EVENTS

1939

Germany invades Poland. France and Britain (called the Allies) declare war on Germany.

1940

Germany invades other parts of Europe. Winston Churchill becomes British Prime Minister. Allied troops are evacuated from Dunkirk on the French coast, in the face of the German advance. Italy joins Germany, declaring war on the Allies.

The Battle of Britain begins between the German Air Force and the British Royal Air Force, and bombing raids on London begin. Japan signs a pact with Germany and Italy. Fighting begins in North Africa between German/Italian and Allied forces.

1941

German troops invade Russia and make gains in North Africa. Japan bombs the US Navy at Pearl Harbor, Hawaii. Germany and Italy declare war on the USA.

1942

The Germans make gains against Allied forces in Africa and advance on the Russian city of Stalingrad. The Japanese invade more territory in the Far East. The Allied Forces attempt a disastrous seaborne attack at Dieppe in France.

In the autumn the war begins to turn in favour of the Allies. The Japanese advance in the Pacific is halted and the Germans are defeated at El Alamein, North Africa. Soviet troops defeat the Germans at Stalingrad.

1943

The German army surrenders at Stalingrad. The Germans and Italians are defeated in North Africa. The Italian dictator Mussolini falls from power and Italy pulls out of the war.

1944

German cities are heavily bombed. On June 6th, known as D-Day, the Allied forces land in Normandy, France to push the German army back across France. There is fierce fighting on all three remaining battle fronts in Europe, Russia and the Far East. The first Allied troops arrive on German soil.

1945

Nazi concentration camp atrocities are discovered, Hitler shoots himself. Germany surrenders and is occupied by the Allied and Russian forces. The USA drops two atomic bombs on Japan and it surrenders. The war is over.

GLOSSARY

Here are some wartime words explained:

ACK-ACK GUNS

Machine guns that were positioned around London to shoot at enemy bombers. Some of these guns were fixed at sites called "batteries". Some were fixed to platforms that could be wheeled around the streets.

AIR RAID

When enemy planes dropped bombs it was called an air raid. When bombers were expected sirens gave a loud signal and people hid inside air-raid shelters.

ALL CLEAR

A signal that meant an air raid was over and people could return to their homes.

ALLIES

All the countries that fought together against Germany, Japan and Italy.

ANDERSON SHELTER

A corrugated iron shelter buried in the garden, with room for six people to sit or sleep inside it. Over two million were issued free by the government for protection during bombing raids.

A.R.P. WARDEN

A.R.P. stands for Air Raid Precautions. Volunteer A.R.P. wardens patrolled their local area, checking that lights were out at night and taking charge of people in emergencies.

ATOMIC BOMB

A nuclear bomb. The first nuclear weapon was dropped on Japan by the Allies on August 6th, 1945. It killed 70,000 people in the city of Hiroshima. On August 9th a second nuclear bomb was dropped on Nagasaki, forcing Japan to surrender.

AXIS POWERS

Germany and her wartime partners Italy and Japan.

BARRAGE BALLOONS

Large airborne balloons that were tethered above the ground to block the path of enemy planes.

BATTLE OF BRITAIN

Fighting in the air between the RAF and the German Luftwaffe (air force) between July and November 1940. Hitler wanted to gain mastery of the skies over Britain before he sent his troops to invade, but by the end of 1940 he had lost so many planes he postponed the planned invasion.

BLACK MARKETEER

Someone who broke the law by selling stolen goods that were supposed to be rationed, for instance, petrol or food.

BLACKOUT

During the war the blackout was law in Britain. It meant that outside lighting was switched off and indoor lighting was hidden behind blackout curtains, so that enemy planes would find it hard to pinpoint targets at night.

BLITZ

The night-time bombing of British cities between September 1940 and May 1941. Industrial cities were targeted, such as London, Coventry, Portsmouth, Southampton, Glasgow, Liverpool, Bristol and Plymouth.

CHURCHILL

Winston Churchill became the British Prime Minister in 1940. He led Britain through the war.

D-DAY

June 6th, 1944, the day when the Allies started to invade the German-occupied territories of Europe. Allied troops landed in Northern France.

ENEMY ALIENS

Ordinary people caught in the wrong country when war began were arrested and imprisoned. For instance, Italians and Germans living in London were regarded as "enemy aliens".

EVACUATION

When children were sent away from their city homes to safer places in the countryside. Evacuation began in September 1939.

GIs

American soldiers, who arrived in Britain in 1942. From their British bases they went off to fight in Europe.

HITLER

Adolf Hitler was the Führer (leader) of Nazi Germany. He led Germany into the war. He killed himself on May 1st 1945.

HOLOCAUST

The imprisonment and murder of many thousands of Jewish people, secretly carried out by the Nazis during their time in power. The true extent of the murders was discovered when Allied troops found the concentration camps where thousands had been imprisoned, starved and killed.

HOME GUARD

Men who could not become full-time soldiers joined the Home Guard and trained as soldiers in their spare time, in case of enemy invasion.

HUN

A word for an enemy German soldier.

INCENDIARY BOMBS

Bombs which did not explode on impact, but instead smouldered and burned, to cause fires. They could be put out with sand, or moved to a safer location. However, some incendiary bombs were booby-trapped so they would explode if they were moved.

JERRY

A nickname for the enemy Germans.

LUFTWAFFE

The German Air Force.

MORRISON SHELTER

A reinforced metal cage which was issued by the government and fitted in homes. The top could be used as a useful table, but during an air raid people could sit inside the cage to protect themselves.

Mussolini

Benito Mussolini,the Italian leader during the war. He was sometimes called Il Duce, which means "the leader".

Nazis

These were members of Hitler's National Socialist Party (also called the Nazi Party). They were in power in Germany during the war.

Prisoner of war camps

Soldiers captured in action were sent to these special prisons. In Germany they were called Stalags. The most famous German prison was Colditz.

Rations

Goods such as petrol, clothes and food were in short supply, so people were only allowed small amounts each. They could only be bought using government coupons which were issued in special books.

Shrapnel

Metal pieces scattered when a bomb explodes.

Stalin

Joseph Stalin, leader of the Soviet Union during the war.

V1s AND V2s

Unmanned German flying bombs first used in 1944. They were driven by an engine, had an automatic pilot, and could fly nearly 260 kilometres (160 miles) to reach a target. V1s made an engine noise that cut out just before the bomb fell, so they were nicknamed "doodle-bugs" or "buzz bombs". V2s were silent.

VE DAY

Victory in Europe Day, May 8th 1945. It was the day when it was officially announced that war with Germany was over.

VJ DAY

Victory in Japan Day, August 16th 1945. It was the day when it was officially announced that war with Japan was over.

Other titles in this series

The diary of a Young Roman Soldier

Young Marcus Gallo is travelling to Britain with his legion to help pacify the wild Celtic tribes. As the Romans march north, Marcus records in his diary how he copes with cold weather, falls in love and narrowly escapes serious injury. Read his diary and find out what life was *really* like for a young Roman soldier.

The diary of a Victorian Apprentice

Young Samuel Cobbett is very excited – he is to be an apprentice at a factory making steam locomotives. Away from the shop floor, Samuel records in his diary how he learns his trade, falls in love and experiences accidents and danger. Read his diary and find out what life was *really* like for a Victorian apprentice.

The diary of a Young Tudor Lady-in-Waiting

Young Rebecca Swann is joining her aunt as a lady-in-waiting at the court of Queen Elizabeth the First. In her secret journal, Rebecca records how she learns to be a courtier, falls in love and uncovers a plot against the Queen. Read her diary and find out what life was *really* like for a young Tudor lady-in-waiting.